This book belongs to

_____

This educational book was created in cooperation with Children's Television Workshop, producers of SESAME STREET. Children do not have to watch the television show to benefit from this book. Workshop revenues from this book will be used to help support CTW educational projects.

ON MY WAY WITH
SESAME STREET™

Volume 9

Cars and Planes, Trucks and Trains

Featuring Jim Henson's Sesame Street Muppets
Children's Television Workshop / Funk & Wagnalls

Authors

Dina Anastasio
Linda Hayward
Valjean McLenighan
Michaela Muntean
Rae Paige
Jessie Smith
Pat Tornborg

Illustrators

Richard Brown
Tom Cooke
Robert Dennis
Joe Ewers
Tom Leigh
Kimberly A. McSparran
Maggie Swanson

0-8343-0083-4   1 2 3 4 5 6 7 8 9 0

A Parents' Guide to CARS AND PLANES, TRUCKS AND TRAINS

Playing truck driver, train engineer, or ship's captain are favorite childhood pastimes. This book of stories and activities about CARS AND PLANES, TRUCKS AND TRAINS is full of information about all the vehicles children love.

"Special Delivery" is an adventure story about Prairie Dawn's Delivery Service. When Ernie hires Prairie Dawn to deliver a package to Bert at the Pigeon Fanciers' Convention, she uses every possible conveyance — from a hot air balloon to a garbage barge — to fulfill her mission.

The story "Going Places" presents Big Bird the airplane pilot, Cookie Monster the train engineer, Ernie the tugboat pilot, and a variety of fascinating vehicles.

"Signs Along the Highway," "What Makes It Go?" and "Oscar in the Harbor" are activities about land and water travel.

"Spacecraft" and "Astro-Bird" give children facts about space travel.

This volume, CARS AND PLANES, TRUCKS AND TRAINS, is the perfect vehicle for finding out how people and things get from one place to another.

The Editors
SESAME STREET BOOKS

SPECIAL DELIVERY

It was Thursday afternoon on Sesame Street. Grover was showing some kids the difference between near and far. Big Bird was cleaning his nest. The Count was counting crates outside Hooper's Store.

Suddenly the phone rang at Prairie Dawn's Delivery Service. She answered on the first ring.

"Can you come over right away?" Ernie asked. "I have something to send Bert. He's gone to a convention and he forgot to take it with him."

"You called the right number," said Prairie Dawn. "We are experts in careful and speedy service."

Prairie Dawn sped off on her skateboard.

"I'm glad I started my own business," she thought as she skipped up the stairs of 123 Sesame Street. "I never know where the next call will take me."

Ernie was in the kitchen tying up a package.

"Put your finger on this knot, will you, please?" he said. "I want to make sure the string is good and tight. This is an important package!"

Ernie pulled out his ink pad and stamped RUSH! on the package in three different places. Next came a HANDLE WITH CARE label, then SPECIAL DELIVERY. There were so many labels on the package that Prairie Dawn could hardly find the address.

"Pinfeather Falls?" she asked in disbelief.

"Yes," said Ernie. "That's where the Pigeon Fanciers' Convention is held. Bert must be frantic without this, so please hurry, Prairie Dawn!"

"Pinfeather Falls," said Prairie Dawn as she unlocked her bike. "That's quite a trip. I guess the first step is to get downtown."

She hopped on her bike and rode off. Suddenly she heard the thwop-thwop-thwopping of a flat tire. "Oops!" she said. "No time to fix it now!"

Prairie Dawn got on a city bus and found a seat next to the window. "There's more than one way to get downtown," she thought.

Suddenly the bus hit a pothole. KA-THUMP! The package bounced out of Prairie Dawn's lap, flew out the window, and landed in the back of a dump truck full of trash.
"Stop!" cried Prairie Dawn.

The bus stopped and she jumped off.

By the time Prairie found a taxi, the truck was almost out of sight.

"Follow that truck!" she said to the taxi driver.

The taxi chased the truck through narrow streets down toward the river. Prairie Dawn could see her package bouncing around on top of the load.

When the taxi turned a corner and pulled up to a dock, the dump truck was already parked and empty.

"It's a good thing Ernie wrapped his package well," said Prairie Dawn as she watched it float down the river on a garbage barge.

Quickly she slipped on a life jacket and jumped into a speedboat at the dock.

Prairie Dawn was halfway to the barge when the speedboat started to slow down. Sputter, sputter! It was out of gas.

Just then she heard a loud noise overhead and looked up to see a hovering helicopter.

The pilot lowered a rope ladder and she climbed up into the helicopter.

"Thanks!" said Prairie Dawn to the pilot. "Just drop me off at the barge, please. And here's my card. Maybe I can make a free delivery for you someday."

"Do you see what I see?" said the captain of the barge to the first mate.

"Ahoy, there! I'm Prairie Dawn of Prairie Dawn's Delivery Service," she said. "I'm here to pick up an important package...and there it is!" she cried, snatching the package from the garbage heap.

"I've never lost a package yet," she said, dusting it off. "Now, if I could just borrow your rowboat, please?"

Prairie Dawn got in the rowboat and rowed as hard as she could toward the shore. When she landed, she ran to the train station—and arrived just in time to catch the 4:17 train to Cooville.

"Whew!" she said when she found a seat on the train. Then she took out her map. There were no railroad tracks or roads between Cooville and Pinfeather Falls.

"Goodness," said Prairie Dawn. "It looks as if the only way to get to Pinfeather Falls from Cooville is as the pigeon flies!"

"Did you say Pinfeather Falls?" asked someone from across the aisle.

"Yes," answered Prairie Dawn. "I must get there right away."

"You are in luck. I am Melba T. Burdbrane, president of the Birds of a Feather Company, and I am on my way to Pinfeather Falls. Would you like to ride with me to the Falls?"

So Prairie Dawn and Melba Burdbrane rode to the convention in a beautiful hot air balloon. The Birds of a Feather flock of homing pigeons guided them to a safe landing in Pinfeather Falls.

"Hey, Bert!" called Prairie Dawn, spotting him in a crowd of pigeon fanciers. "I have a package for you from Ernie."

"Good old Ern!" said Bert, ripping open the package. "He knew I forgot something important."

"What?" gasped Bert. "*A picture of Ernie?* Oh, no. I thought it might be my paper clip collection. I don't leave home without it."

"Sign here, please," said Prairie Dawn.

Traffic Jam in the City

Here come the fire engines! Everyone on the street must pull over to the side to let the fire trucks through. What other trucks do you see?

pickup truck

tank truck

pumper truck

hook-and-ladder truck

pushcart

Grover Rides Again

Which pictures show Grover riding?

Count with the Count

The Count counted seven passengers in the cars. How many cars do you see?

The Count counted eight train cars. Can you count them?

Signs Along the Highway

What Makes It Go?

What makes cars go?
Gasoline.

What makes kids go?
Food.

What makes sailboats go?
Wind.

Going Places

Big Bird's airplane flies way up high in the sky. The town below looks tiny.

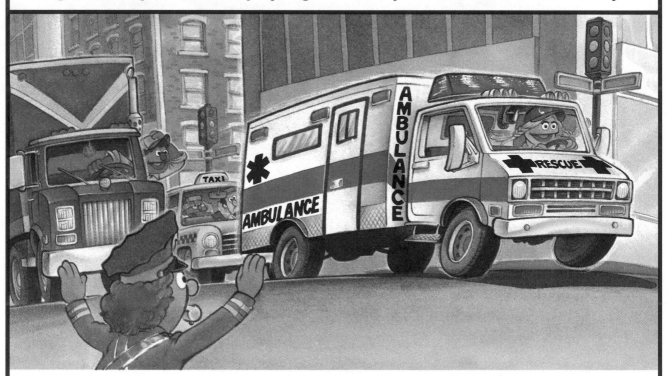

Betty Lou speeds to the hospital in an ambulance. Its red light flashes a warning.

Cookie Monster's train chugs along while a car and a bus wait at the crossing.

The fire truck's siren shrieks, "Rrree—Oooww!" Everyone gets out of the way.

Prairie Dawn catches a speeder in her fast police car. She writes a ticket.

Bert's ferryboat carries people and cars back and forth all day long.

Rodeo Rosie's Jeep bounces over the sandy range. Watch out, cows!

Ernie's tugboat pushes the big ocean liner into port. Toot, toot!

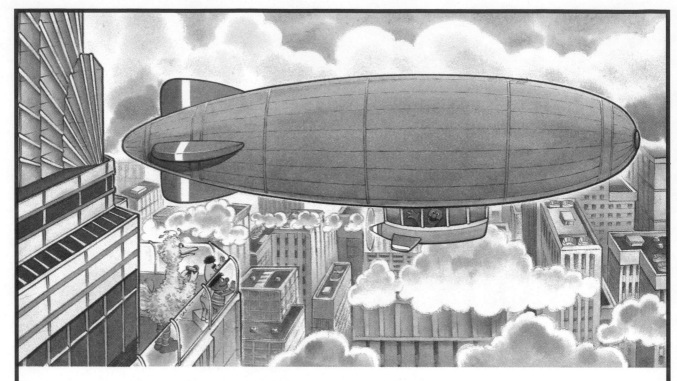

Grover's blimp glides over the city. Everyone waves.

Herry Monster drives uptown, downtown, across town, and around town in the Sesame Street bus. He takes people where they want to go.

Working Together

Big Bird is watching the new apartment building going up on Sesame Street. Can you name the work machines?

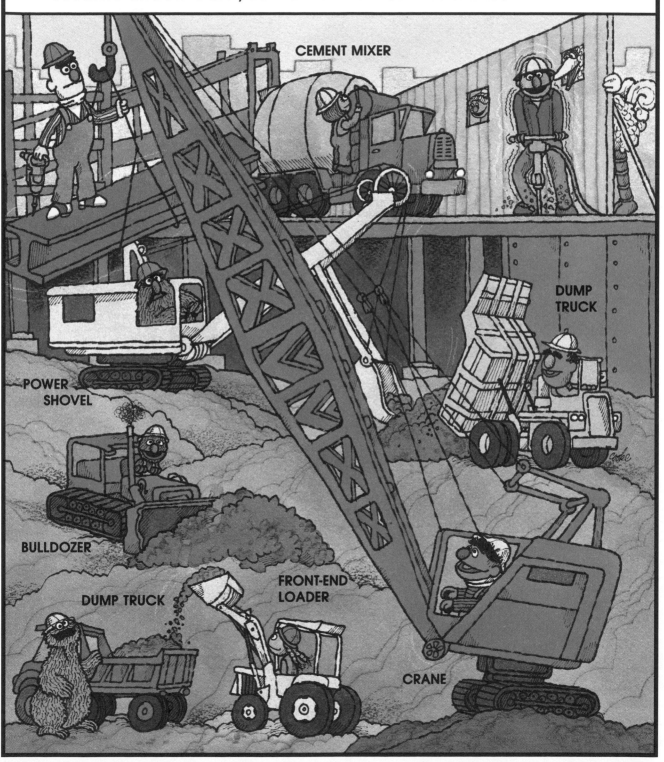

Oscar in the Harbor

Oscar is going on a vacation cruise. His friends have come to say good-bye. What boat would you like to ride on?

buoy

lighthouse

sailboat

jetty

oil tanker

floating derrick

pilothouse

lifeboat

fireboat

pilings

POLICE

police boat

ferryboat

cargo hoist

forklift truck

warehouse

cargo

hold

PIER 6

tractor-trailer truck

container ship

GROVER'S FLIGHT OF FANCY

The sky sometimes seems like a big bowl of fruit
That is waiting for me. Oh, it all looks so cute!
The moon is a grapefruit, a juicy delight.
The sun is an orange; I'm taking a bite.

I dream that my plane is a big silver spoon,
And I'm eating a chunk of that beautiful moon.
The whole thing is gone after three or four trips,
And the people shout, "There's a total eclipse!"

Then I sprinkle a planet with handfuls of stars,
And I circle around for a nibble of Mars!
When I come back to earth from this wonderful flight,
I have a headful of dreams, and a big appetite!

Note: Adult supervision is suggested.

Sun Jelly Sundae

To serve four—

What you need:
1 envelope of unflavored gelatin
¾ cup of cold water
1 can of frozen orange juice concentrate, just thawed
½ cup of very cold water
3 mandarin orange sections

What you do:
Pour ¾ cup of cold water into a saucepan, and sprinkle in the gelatin. Stir it over low heat for 3 minutes, just until it melts. Turn off the heat, and let the gelatin cool for about 5 minutes. Pour in the orange juice concentrate. Stir in the ½ cup of very cold water. Then pour it all into a mold or round-bottomed bowl. Put it in the refrigerator.

After about half an hour, when the gel is partly set, push the orange sections all the way down to the bottom of the bowl. That way they will come out on top when the gelatin is unmolded. Leave the mold in the refrigerator until you are ready to serve it, or for at least another hour. Unmold the Sun Jelly.

Full-Moon Salads

Follow the Sun Jelly recipe, but use frozen grapefruit juice concentrate instead of orange juice, and pieces of pineapple ring instead of orange sections. Mold the gel in 4 small, round-bottomed bowls so that each person has a full moon.

When the gel is partly set, press the pieces of pineapple ring to the bottom to make the eyes and mouth. Unmold the moons onto 4 salad plates spread with lettuce. If you like, put several chunks of avocado on each plate.

Find the Trucks

Find these trucks in the picture. Point to them.

What is each truck doing in the neighborhood?

Big Bird at the Airport

weather instruments

air traffic controller

runway

passenger terminal

cargo plane

control tower

cargo loader

pilot

propeller plane

cargo

WELCOME GRANNY BIRD!

guardrail

observation deck

Granny Bird is coming for a visit. Big Bird and Maria are picking her up at the airport. Have you ever flown on an airplane?

radar antenna

hangars

ACE AVIATION INC.

windsock

helicopter

fire truck

fuel truck

tail

food-service truck

jet passenger plane 47201

copilot

flight engineer

passenger

flight attendant

wing

captain

baggage

baggage handler

mechanic

baggage train

passenger stairs

Spacecraft

What is LEM?

The Lunar Excursion Module (LEM) is the name of the spacecraft that actually landed on the moon.

What is a space station?

Space stations are laboratories that can be sent into space.

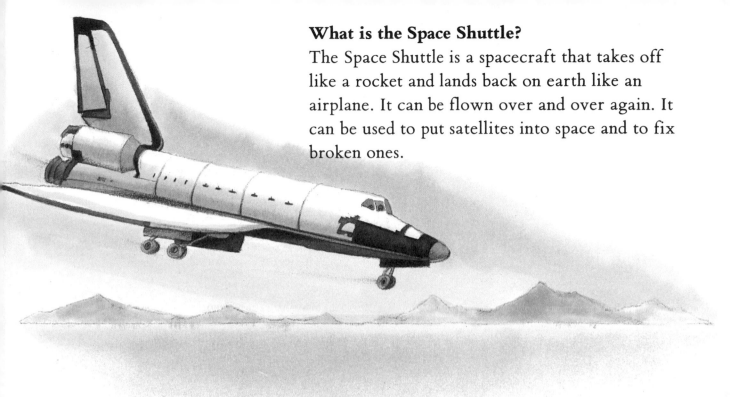

What is the Space Shuttle?

The Space Shuttle is a spacecraft that takes off like a rocket and lands back on earth like an airplane. It can be flown over and over again. It can be used to put satellites into space and to fix broken ones.

What is a satellite?

A satellite is a machine that is launched into space by a rocket or the Space Shuttle. Different satellites do different kinds of work. Some send television pictures from one part of the world to another.

Astro-Bird

Look at me, everybody!
I'm an astro-bird!

What are astronauts?
They are space explorers
who blast off to outer
space in spacecraft.

Why do astronauts wear spacesuits?
Because they have to take their own air with
them. Spacesuits supply the astronauts with air,
and, like big snowsuits, also keep them warm.

Blast-off

Ten, nine, eight, seven, six,
five, four, three, two,
one...BLAST OFF!

Astronauts do not weigh anything
when they are in space. If they don't
wear their seat belts they float around
in the spacecraft.